BOURBON BACHELOR

A Bourbon Canyon Novella

WALKER ROSE

LE Publishing

I won a date with the most eligible bachelor in Bourbon Canyon—except I wasn't the one bidding.

Two of my best friends dragged me to a fundraiser and bid in my place. Tate Bailey isn't just some mountain man bachelor the rest of town gushes about. He's also the dad of one of my most troublesome fourth-grade students.

My only dealings with the divorced bourbon empire heir have been outlining the issues his son is having in school. Not exactly the best first impression—or second, third, and fourth.

The last thing I want is another rundown of everything my exes say is wrong with me, especially from a rugged guy like Tate. But when I tell him he's off the hook, he insists.

Fine. It's only a date. Then I can go back to my dull life with my heart intact. Because there's no way a guy like Tate would give up his bachelorhood for a boring, predictable, small-town teacher like me.

Copyright © 2023 by Walker Rose

Editing by Razor Sharp Editing

Proofreading by My Brother's Editor, Deaton Author Services, Judy's Proofreading, and Fairy Proofmother Proofreading

Cover art by Okay Creations

All rights reserved.

No part of this book may be reproduced in any form or by any electronic or mechanical means, including information storage and retrieval systems, without written permission from the author, except for the use of brief quotations in a book review.

The characters, places, and events in this story are fictional. Any similarities to real people, places, or events are coincidental and unintentional.

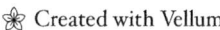 Created with Vellum

Scarlett

The first atrocity my two best friends committed was dragging me out on a Friday night. Bourbon Canyon's population was in the low four figures. Except for the occasional street dance, football game, or Fourth of July fireworks show, there wasn't anything to do on a Friday night. Even when there were events in town, I sat them out and happily tucked myself into the corner of the couch with my embroidery and murder shows.

Since I'd been single, I'd been impossible to guilt about my nonsocial adventures.

After a week of teaching a bustling class of rambunctious fourth graders, my sole focus was a quiet night. No negotiations. No standardized testing. No playground arguments over balls, whose turn it was, or who cut in line.

Summer break started last week, and though I

tutored over summer vacation, the personal recharge was still valid.

The second atrocity Summer Kerrigan and her sister Autumn committed was bringing me to Bourbon Canyon's Fifth Annual Bachelor Auction.

"Ladies, the auction is about to begin," the announcer called through the church's sound system.

Because didn't all bachelor auctions take place where babies were baptized?

The auction was a fundraiser for the local food pantry and children's resource center. Bourbon Canyon wasn't the only town to participate, and the proceeds were distributed throughout the county. If I had money to donate, I'd have indulged.

Maybe.

I shoved my glasses up my nose. Probably not. I'd rather write a check and keep my pride intact. After what my last ex had said about me, no doubt the whole town thought I needed to buy a guy in order to date.

"Come on, Scarlett. We need a back-row seat." Summer's strawberry-blond hair fell over her shoulder as she nudged me toward a pew. People streamed around us to take a seat and watch the show. Was everyone here going to bid?

"Why?" I asked.

"So I can see who's bidding." Summer grinned at me, then bit her lip as her gaze skated toward the front. The bachelors would get marched out one by one. Did she have a bachelor in mind? Or did Autumn? Summer was the only one who'd registered for a bidding paddle. When we entered the church, she'd beelined to the auction table. A large *84* was emblazoned across the homemade cardboard bidding paddle.

Autumn slid in on the other side of me, sandwiching me in. She patted her auburn hair like she was nervous. Was there someone she also didn't want to see auctioned off?

The whole thing was kitschy, but I had to admit the energy buzzing through the room was good-natured and fun.

Women of all ages were here, but not for the reasons one would think. The bachelor auction didn't just put single men up for bid. Married guys offered their services for a day and those skills didn't include romantic dinners and long walks. Only a few bachelors were actually offering a date.

Tate Bailey was one of them.

Summer and Autumn's oldest brother. The four Kerrigan sisters were adopted. And while all three of their Bailey brothers were handsome, Tate was a standout, *in my modest opinion*.

A month ago, when I'd heard he'd agreed to do the auction, I'd fantasized for an entire week. I'd gone to school and had a hard time looking his son in the eye. The things I'd dreamed of doing to Tate Bailey…

A girl could dream, but one of my best traits was being realistic. Which was why I had wanted to stay far away from this year's auction. I had only seen Tate when it was to inform him of the trouble his son Chance had gotten into. Tate had a glower that could incinerate the panties off a girl in all the best ways, but when it was aimed at me, my granny panties wanted to hang their head in shame.

I couldn't cater to my infatuation with Tate. I'd been his kid's fourth-grade teacher, and for nine months, I'd felt like the biggest tattletale alive while facing down those intimidating, narrowed eyes and big, bulging crossed arms.

While I was technically no longer Chance's teacher, I didn't delude myself. When Tate strode through town, I'd actually heard women sigh. He towered over me by a good eight inches, which was probably less than what was in his pants. But to that man, I'd be nothing but Miss Scarlett Breen, Chance's picky teacher.

Before Tate had moved back to town, I would've claimed the whole mountain man thing wasn't my type. Then I'd seen him in his worn jeans, cowboy boots, and flannels. Now I was a convert.

Half the allure was knowing he had a brain. He used to run the headquarters of his family's Copper Summit Bourbon Distillery in Bozeman before he moved home.

Autumn had shown me a picture of his ex-wife. She was my opposite. I didn't believe in rating people by their looks, but dammit, she was a ten. I was a...six. If I rounded up. Average, from my hair to my height to my clothes.

Even tonight, I was in jean capris and a yellow shirt with walking sandals. Autumn wasn't dressed much differently, only she wore flip-flops. I needed more arch support. Summer dressed like her name. Light, flouncy summer dresses and wedge sandals that I'd break an ankle in.

A lady approached the podium with the mic. Wilna Whitecloud. She worked in the church office, ran the local animal shelter, and was involved in every Bourbon Canyon shindig possible. The auction was her brainchild.

She tapped the mic, and the thud rang through the chapel. "Everyone's about seated. All right. We'll go ahead and get started." She clasped her hands in front of her. "Welcome to the fifth annual Bourbon Canyon Bachelor Auction, where our bachelors are as stiff as our drinks."

I coughed on a laugh. Summer giggled next to me and Autumn pinched the bridge of her nose. I'd rather be at the bar and grill downtown than here. It wasn't often the three of us could get together. Autumn was a teacher at the same school as me, but Summer lived and worked in Bozeman at the family distillery.

"She'll never get tired of that joke," Autumn muttered.

The distillery had gotten its start in Bourbon Canyon with the Baileys' grandparents, hence the name of the town. And hence Wilna's joke.

The first bachelor was up. He was the janitor at the church and the elementary school, married, and auctioning off his handyman skills. An older couple that lived on a ranch outside of city limits won his bid for an amount that made me choke.

Damn. How much would Tate go for?

How much did I have in the bank?

No. *No.*

I wasn't here to bid. I didn't have a paddle. That was that.

Another guy walked to the podium. A local cop who had offered a day of yard work.

Maybe I should've bid. My lawn was in bad shape, and I had an acrimonious relationship with my lawn mower.

Could he fix roofs?

Didn't matter. The whole no-money thing was the deciding factor.

With each auction, Wilna ran her finger down a list to check attendees' names against their paddle numbers before calling out the winner. She could name each person in the audience *and* when they'd been born, but she'd always been a stickler for routine.

Summer bounced her leg next to me. Was she nervous? Did she have her eye on a *bachelor* bachelor? She'd never mentioned having the hots for anyone in town.

After seven men had been bid on and won, Tate walked up to the podium. My heart rate kicked up. He'd kept to his jeans-and-flannel look. His green-plaid shirt lightened his dark eyes. The way he clasped his hands in front of him looked casual, but tension rode across his shoulders.

I almost felt guilty for visually devouring him while no one could see. Everyone's eyes were on him.

What a dessert. I could lick him upside down and sideways.

But he wasn't mine. He'd be some other girl's lucky date.

Would he take them to the bar and grill? Or out to the massive cabin he'd built on family land? Did he have some epically romantic ideas in mind, or was he the type to pick up a girl, doze through a movie, then expect her to put out after his minimal effort?

I was projecting. A mediocre date with Tate would probably blow my best date out of the water, but then it wasn't hard to win over the one that had ended with "Babe, you sure you want to add a dessert onto what you just ate?"

I studied all the single women in the crowd, my jealousy ratcheting up. My attention caught on a few married ladies tapping their paddles against their hands. This could get ugly.

Tate Bailey might be worth it.

When he'd moved back to town, the chatter had been unhinged. Star high school football wide receiver. Valedictorian. Big brother to "all those poor kids"—his foster siblings. He had two biological brothers too, but Tate was the mystery. He'd moved away after high school, earned his degree, and worked at the main distillery, and then when his dad had gotten sick, he'd come home to take over the ranch. Local golden boy swoops back home to roost.

"Tate Bailey is our last bachelor. He's offering a date —an entire day and on into the evening for the winner." Wilna's grin was wide. Dollar signs were in her eyes. "Open bid."

"One thousand!" a woman yelled from the front, her paddle waving in the air with a number one. Had she camped outside before the doors opened?

Wilna knew the woman's name, but she checked her sheet once again. "One thousand from Hannah Kline."

"Fifteen hundred." Another woman brandished her paddle.

"Sixteen hundred."

"Eighteen."

"Two."

Two thousand dollars for a date with Tate Bailey?

God, I'd pay that just to stare at him for a couple of hours without being creepy.

Nah. It'd still be creepy.

"Twenty-five." This was from another couple. Ah, the Olsons. Knowing them, they weren't looking for yard work either.

"Twenty-six," Hannah said, less confident this time. "Twenty-nine."

My mind spun, listening to the bids. But relief flowed through me too. I'd harbored a secret crush on Tate, and if I'd come here to bid on him, I would've been wiped out after the first bid.

Following the relief was a dismal cloud settling in. He'd go on a date. Everyone would talk about it. Then he'd go on more. He'd been in town for a year and hadn't been out beyond running errands and taking his kid to the bar and grill, but people talked about his prowess "back in the day." They also discussed his postdivorce love life before he'd moved into his mountain cabin on his family's land. Apparently, it was juicy enough to ride the small-town grapevine the forty miles from Bozeman to Bourbon Canyon.

I let out a long sigh. The bids were up to five grand.

Could I leave mid-bidding war? Claim I had to use the bathroom and walk home to my small rental house? A documentary on a serial killer would be better than watching the guy I'd dreamed about walking out with another woman.

Hannah rallied and shouted, "Ten thousand!"

Silence fell. I thought the first guy going for eight hundred was obscene—yet quite generous. This was for charity. If I kept that thought forefront in my mind, maybe I wouldn't consume my weight in chocolate-covered almonds tonight.

"Ten thousand to Hannah!" Wilna scanned the audience. "Going once..."

Summer brandished her paddle. "Eleven."

What? Everyone had turned to stare at us, but I kept my head down. I was used to a class of kids eyeing me.

But anyone else and I wanted to melt through the floor. It'd been worse since my breakup two years ago.

My ex's words rang in my mind. *You're just...uninspiring.*

Summer's foot bobbed up and down, the only sign all the attention was getting to her.

Was she trying to get her brother to be her bitch for a day?

I snuck a peek at the front. Tate's dark brows were drawn together, and he was giving his sister a *What the hell?* look.

Wilna beamed. "Eleven—"

"Twelve," Hannah snapped before Wilna could finish.

"Fifteen," Summer countered.

Hannah's nostrils flared. "S-sixteen."

I almost felt bad for her. She wasn't a mean person, but she was forward, especially with the men in town, which didn't make her a fan of their significant others.

Summer fanned her paddle in the air. "*Twen-ty*," she said in a singsong voice like she could bid all night.

"Oh. Say." Wilna tapped her fingers together like hundred-dollar bills were falling from the sky. They sort of were. "Twenty thousand. Going once... Going twice... Sold. Tate Bailey to..." She ran her finger down her chart of names.

"Scarlett Breen."

Tate

. . .

My stunned gaze went from my sister to the woman shrinking into the bench next to her.

Scarlett Breen.

Miss Scarlett.

No one called her Miss Breen. Chance had called her a different name once, and I'd made him shovel shit from one side of the manure pile to the other for a week straight.

Had I seen incorrectly? Hadn't my sister been the one bidding? I'd had no clue why, and I had dreaded finding out. The sister who'd put worms in my bed couldn't be trusted.

But Wilna didn't call out Summer Kerrigan as the winner.

Miss Scarlett.

After the way fourth grade had begun, I'd feared she'd declare Chance unfit, but she'd reassured me the second time she'd called me into her classroom for a parent-teacher meeting that his behavior was normal and he was improving. He'd started out hating her, then it had faded to animosity and, finally, apathy. Chance didn't *not* like Miss Scarlett.

I didn't know what she thought about me, but I'd started out the year wanting to toss her over my shoulder, take her to a dark room, and see if I could soften those pert lips into a breathless gasp.

I'd ended the year stroking off to the image.

Miss Scarlett would live up to her name if she knew my dirty thoughts about her. No one knew the little teacher who wore cardigans and long skirts or boring slacks filled up Tate Bailey's spank bank.

And the way she refused to meet my eyes when she was done talking about Chance ground into me like road rash. Something about me intimidated her, and if just being myself scared her, I was better off keeping my thoughts about her in my head.

"Twenty thousand. That's a record." The tiny grandma running the auction glowed. Wilna had stopped to talk to me in the grocery store one day and the conversation had somehow ended with me doing this damn auction. "Enjoy your date with Miss Scarlett."

My gaze shot to the pretty teacher. Summer and Autumn flanked her on either side, shit-eating grins in place, but Scarlett's horrified gaze was on me.

Well. Damn.

I nodded at her. She jerked, her gaze flying to the floor, her face beet red.

Summer had been bidding, and from Scarlett's expression, it wasn't a long jump to figure out what had happened. My sister had bid for Scarlett without telling her.

Did she know something I didn't?

The way Scarlett was melting into the pew said no. Miss Scarlett had not planned to bid on me, not in this auction or any other.

Wilna ushered me off. I stayed with the other bachelors in what I'd dubbed "the corral," a small room off the main chapel with chairs and tables used for meetings or Bible study. The bachelors were supposed to wait for our winners to come claim us.

People trickled in, all of them looking me over. Some of them threw a "nice job" my way as if I'd done more than stand on a stage and breathe.

Twenty grand.

What the hell did you do, Summer?

My fucking family.

I loved my sisters, but one bonus of being the oldest was that I'd gotten to move away sooner and escape my siblings' drama.

The bachelors filtered out after making arrangements with their winners, but I waited. Alone.

Damn.

Finally, Summer appeared in the doorway, a grimace on her face.

I folded my arms, glad I hadn't worn a suit to this mess. "You didn't tell her your grand plan, did you?"

She winced and edged inside. "She has a thing for you. I know it."

Miss Scarlett? "She's had a year to give me one sign of interest, but she won't look at me if it's not about Chance."

Her expression said *duh*. "Do you know why she won't look at you?" She shoved my arm. "Hello? She likes you."

My doubt held firm. "That doesn't give you the right to embarrass her."

She leaned in. "I don't hear you saying you don't like her."

"Why would I say that?" I liked her more than I should. I'd written off marriage after my divorce, but a woman like Scarlett Breen could make a guy think.

Her answering smile was triumphant. "Before you ask—and I know you will—we pooled the cash."

"Who?"

"Me and the others."

"How many of the others?"

A smile played over her lips. How could someone so petite jerk a big guy like me around? She'd done it since she'd arrived on my family's doorstep. "Autumn,

Wynter, and June. Tenor and Teller threw in some cash too."

My brothers had probably contributed the most, knowing I couldn't get mad at my sisters like I could with them. "Why the fuck would you do that?"

"First, it's a tax write-off." She held up two fingers. My diminutive sister had never been intimidated by me, not even when she'd first come to the ranch as a traumatized little girl. "And second, because you've been a moody recluse since you moved here."

"There's nothing wrong with that."

"Chance needs a woman in his life, or he's going to be scratching his balls and peeing by the mailbox every day."

"I only did that once."

Her look said she didn't believe me. "And I happened to drive up at that exact time? Sure."

"Chance has his mother."

"Who gave you custody because she travels too much for work."

True. "He has aunts."

"Autumn is the only one who lives in town, and Junie travels a lot."

"It's enough."

"Not for you. You don't need to grow into an old, cranky man all by yourself in the mountains."

"I like it that way." If I couldn't be in the city doing the job that had become my identity, then I was fine as a moody recluse.

"We don't. It's breaking Daddy's heart."

Summer was a crafty pain in my ass. She always knew what to say to get me to do what she wanted. Dad didn't like that I'd upended my life to move home and help him. Nothing said sick more than giving up his ranching duties and his work in the original Bailey Distillery in Bourbon Canyon. "Fine. Say I do this—"

"For charity. Twenty grand, Tate."

I ignored her. Ultimately, the decision to fulfill my duties wasn't up to me. "What if Scarlett doesn't want a date with me?"

"She does." She put her hand up when I opened my mouth. "Trust me. A woman knows." At my dubious look, she dropped her hand. "Pretend she does have a thing for you. Would you go on a date with her?"

I wanted to do more than date her. I wanted to know if the sweet teacher had dirty thoughts. I wanted to find out how creamy her skin was under her layered clothes. I wanted to bury myself inside that soft body and stay that way until the sun rose.

"Yeah," I said gruffly.

Autumn popped her head in the doorway. "I couldn't hold on to her. She's walking home."

Stark fear passed through Summer's face. My sisters really wanted this. She grabbed my arm. "You have to talk her into it. I swear I'm not wrong. If you like her at all, convince her to give it a shot."

I didn't move. I wasn't going to force my presence on her.

"Twenty grand," Summer stressed as if I wasn't as stunned as the rest of tonight's guests at the amount.

"If you two don't do this, it'll look bad for her, not you," Autumn added.

Fuck me, she was right. This town put me on a pedestal I hadn't earned. I worked as hard as the next guy, but I was a third-generation Bailey and that garnered its own respect. Scarlett was a Bourbon

Canyon transplant and wouldn't be given the same pass. People would think something was wrong with her and not me.

"Fine," I grumbled like this entire day was a nuisance when really the pounding need to get to Scarlett before she disappeared into her tidy little house spurred me on.

I was out of the church and in my truck in no time. I pulled out of the parking lot, nodding at the church as if thanking it for Bourbon Canyon being a small town. I knew where everyone lived. Mostly. I might pay special attention to quiet but stern teachers with round asses I wanted to sink my teeth into.

I spotted Scarlett marching down the sidewalk away from the church with her arms swinging. The nice butt she was probably oblivious to was rolling under the denim.

I lowered the passenger window and slowed. "Miss Scarlett."

She stiffened and glanced over. The way her mouth was pursed would make me behave in a heartbeat. No wonder she'd tamed my wild son in only a handful of months.

"It was a misunderstanding." She continued walking, staring straight ahead. "Sorry for the trouble."

"My sister told me what she did." I didn't have to clarify which sister. Summer was usually a shit starter. Autumn was a lot like Scarlett. A mellow rule follower. "Look, you still won the bid."

She shook her head but still kept her gaze off me. And didn't that get under my skin. I wanted her eyes on me. I wanted her attention on me. I wanted her under me.

Goddammit. Me and my painful boner were going to

scare the pretty teacher off if I leered at her while I followed her in my pickup.

Her arms swung. Her feet stomped in her comfortable hiking sandals. "I had no part in the bidding."

I rode the brake, idling in time with her. We had three blocks before she reached her house. "So you don't want to go on a date with me?"

"No!" She looked over, her expression horrified. "I-I mean, no offense—"

"Offense taken, Miss Scarlett. Twenty thousand dollars, and you don't want to go out with me? I'd hate for Wilna to give the money back because I didn't fulfill my duty."

That got her to stop. I pressed the brake all the way. She puffed a lock of golden-brown hair out of her face and shifted her weight from foot to foot. "You're giving the money back?"

"It wasn't made as a straight donation."

Uncertainty fluttered across her face. I willed her not to look too deeply at the rules. I had no fucking clue. I just needed to convince her to be with me for the day.

"How 'bout I stop by tomorrow?" Suddenly, I didn't want to wait another day to find out what Scarlett Breen was like to date.

"Tomorrow?" She blinked big amber eyes behind her glasses.

I propped an arm on the steering wheel, not giving one shit whether I blocked the middle of the narrow residential road. "I can come by around ten o'clock. That'd give me time to take Chance to Mom and Dad's."

I'd promised him we'd go fishing on Sunday, but I could pick him up from my parents' Sunday morning and go straight to our secret fishing spot on the lake on our property.

She jolted like my words carried an electrical current. "Ten? In the morning?"

"Twenty grand for a whole-day date." I couldn't stop the wolfish grin that slipped out.

Her eyes went wider. Christ, but I bet she was responsive. I'd bet another twenty grand she was one of the quiet ones who didn't hold back when they slammed into their peak.

"The entire day?" She glanced around, but the girl was alone to endure my attention. I rather liked it. "W-what are we going to do?"

Goddamn, Miss Scarlett.

Instead of skittering away from what had to be a hungry look on my face, she narrowed her eyes. "Are you messing with me, Tate?"

Tate. That one got me. She had always referred to me as Mr. Bailey, and I liked the way Miss Scarlett slipped between my lips. Silky and smooth.

"I'd never mess with you, Miss Scarlett."

She rolled her eyes. "You can just call me Scarlett. I'm not Chance's teacher anymore."

"I wish you were. You were amazing with him."

She lifted a shoulder like it was no big deal, but it was. My son had been switched from classroom to classroom in Bozeman. "So, tomorrow? What do you do for a date for the entire day?"

Had she never been taken out for more than dinner? "What do you need done?" Yeah, I let suggestion infuse my voice.

Those innocent, yet somehow shrewd, eyes narrowed once again. "I need my lawn mowed."

I wasn't a Day of Work Bachelor. I was a Date Bachelor, but if it would get her to open her door to me, then I'd take it. "I'll mow your lawn."

"And my roof has a leak."

"Wet things don't stand a chance around me."

Her face bloomed red, and she pressed her fingers to her forehead. "Do you know how you sound?"

The woman could only be pushed so far. I went for honesty. "The truth is, I'd like to get to know you. Take the date. I know my sisters pissed you off, but you and I can enjoy ourselves." Saying *that* without sounding like a turned-on prick was difficult.

"They didn't upset me." She glanced away. "It's embarrassing."

"Think how it'd hurt my poor reputation if you didn't let me take you out."

Another eye roll and a disbelieving smirk. I hadn't gotten this side of her when she'd met with me about my son. I'd gotten the stern teacher with a firm hand for a kid who felt like his mother didn't want him and his father was too busy for him.

"All right," she finally said. "Be at my house at ten."

I was going to push my luck, but I wanted to get to the date side of the bachelor win. "I'll take a look at that roof too. Then, for supper, you can come out to my place and I'll make you some Bailey Beef T-bones."

"I'm a vegetarian."

I nearly gasped. I was a rancher's kid, a rancher who ran one of the biggest distilleries in the state. Bourbon and beef were in my blood.

Her laughter rang out, and she pressed a hand to her chest. "Just kidding."

I huffed out a laugh, but my blood heated. Scarlett

had a hidden side, and I planned to uncover every inch of it. "It'd be fine if you were. I'd just have a lot less to work with at home, and the grocery store's closed."

"You've got a lot to work with, Tate Bailey. That's what I'm afraid of," she murmured. "Let's go to Canyon Grill instead so you can fulfill the dating part."

Was she afraid of me or afraid to be alone with me? Curly's Canyon Grill was the most public a person could get on a Saturday night in Bourbon Canyon. "If you need a public spot, then Curly's will work." Though it wouldn't be her in my home, getting her sweet frosted-sugar-cookie scent all over my house.

She gave me a small parting smile and kept walking. "See you tomorrow."

I tapped my fingers on the steering wheel. "See you bright and early, Miss Scarlett." I drove away and tried not to hit parked cars while I watched her swaying walk in the rearview mirror.

A date.

I'd been divorced for five years. I wasn't bitter about it, and I'd been on dates, but they hadn't been for a relationship. There'd been no end goal. Chance complained about not getting enough time with me. I couldn't take more from him. So when my place had been finished in Bourbon Canyon, we'd moved, and I hadn't dated since. Chance deserved my time.

My ex had always chosen her career over a family, and I'd known it when we married. I should've known how it would go, but I'd been too focused on ticking all the boxes. Work for the family business—check. Get married—check. Have two point five kids—almost check.

I hadn't thought about trying a real relationship

again since I'd signed on the dotted line that ended my last one.

Scarlett made me think again. She made me picture a cozy home full of love and chaos, like the place I'd grown up in.

It figured that the woman who opened my mind to what-ifs was the one woman my son would say "absolutely not" to.

Scarlett

Tate Bailey was on my roof. He'd arrived at 9:55 a.m.

I'd been ready since eight. I'd dressed in a loose fuchsia skirt that I wore on not-so-windy days to keep from flashing the playground my underwear collection. The skirt's dark color helped to hide the yellow polka dots I'd worn today to bolster my confidence.

Other women went to the gym, got highlights, maybe had their nails done. I got fun, quirky underclothes no one would ever see.

Tate wasn't seeing them today. I knew that much.

I still couldn't believe he'd invited me to his place. His mountain cabin on the outskirts of his family's land had been the talk of the break room on more than one occasion. Between the single—and some married— teachers and interns, Tate Bailey had been the center of much break-room speculation on who he'd been out with since he'd been back to town.

No one. And I wasn't the only one who'd noticed.

I was just one of the few who didn't join in on the talk.

I listened, though. *Avidly*.

And now I was on a date with him.

Did fixing my roof really count as a date?

He wasn't even on the ground like I was. I bent over my flower beds, pulling weeds and getting my unmanicured nails dirty. Ugh. I'd showered this morning, but I already needed another one. I hadn't been able to sit in the house while Tate was working.

He'd mowed the lawn in diagonal rows. My neat little yard looked like a checkerboard. And then he'd edged the sidewalk and flower beds. He dumped out bags of landscaping rocks and raked them out. And now he was fixing the roof that my landlord kept saying he'd get to. I should've cleared the work first, but maybe I could negotiate my rent down for a month.

That wouldn't be right. I couldn't take money for work Tate did. I could donate it to the same charities the auction had been for. Yeah. I'd do that since Tate was functioning as a two-for-one bachelor.

I shouldn't have turned down going to his house.

I shook my head and tugged another weed. Sweat dotted my brow and my stomach growled. The sandwiches I'd made for the lunch he'd stuffed into his mouth before going to the roof had long burned off.

I didn't hate yard work. I just wasn't used to a behemoth of a man joining me and making it look more effortless than paint-by-numbers.

I pushed my hair off my forehead and got a wrist full of sweat. Sophisticated as always.

"Looking good."

I straightened. His voice came from above me. I squinted up at him. "What?"

"The flower beds." He grinned as if that wasn't what he'd meant.

Not for the first time since last night, I got the impression he was flirting with me. I didn't buy it. I'd heard too much about him from his sisters. He was honorable. A man like Tate would want to make sure the twenty grand was well spent. He'd want me to have a good time and enjoy myself, to feel special even. But he wasn't flirting because I was special to him.

"Oh. Thanks. My mom gave me the peonies last year, and the hollyhocks came with the house." Could I sound more undesirable? How many of Tate's women had waxed on about their flower beds?

"I'm almost done."

How red was my face? The temperature was approaching eighty, and I burned as easily as I blushed. "Okay. I'll get us something to drink."

I took my trowel and hoe to the garage and tucked them into their place. Summer teased me about my penchant for organization, but she didn't get it. Autumn might, but just because we were teachers didn't mean we coped the same. The mower and gas can were sitting wonky, so I adjusted those too.

A wall of heat hit my back, and my entire body went into blush mode. He was behind me. I spun around.

"Sorry." His self-effacing smirk was a change from the grim dad I'd met with. The whole day, he'd been a different person. Casual. Lighter. Last night too. "I was going to put everything back when I finished."

"It's not a problem. I just like...order."

He flashed a quick smile, and I had to skate my gaze

away. He wore simple jeans, cowboy boots, and a tight gray T-shirt with sweat stains. Manly sweat stains. Not like mine. I looked like I should get my blood pressure checked. Maybe have my cholesterol tested.

"I imagine it's necessary when working with all those kids."

Shock swept through me. My ex had complained about my need for a calm home when work could be chaotic. "Well, in a way. Mostly because my classroom can get disorderly, I like to come home and have everything in its spot. Simple. No thought. Then, when I'm at work, I can let the chaos go."

He brushed his forehead with the back of his arm. The guy made pit sweat sexy too, though his bronzed forearms and biceps stole the show. And the way his abdomen tapered into his hips and his jeans hung low—

"Makes sense."

He was watching me. And I was ogling him. The corners of his eyes crinkled. He *knew* I found him attractive. Not like it was a surprise. Not many people said, *You know that Tate Bailey? He should take some care with his appearance.*

I'd had that said about me enough.

"My ex used to have a hard time when Chance was a baby. She was used to traveling and doing her own thing on her own schedule, and you can't do that with a baby."

"Chance took it hard, didn't he?"

He nodded, his throat working. "Harder than I thought. I mean, Tamera loves him, don't get me wrong. But she knew I was the better full-time parent. I knew it too."

"Kids aren't so matter of fact." I toed the half-empty gas can into its spot. The fumes briefly blocked out his fresh mountain air scent. Was that an aftershave, or was even his smell that good?

"Exactly. Listen, I'll put the ladder and tools away, then do you mind going to Canyon Grill early?"

My heart stopped. Of course he wanted to cut the date short—

"Then we can go for a walk by the river or something."

Happiness coursed through me, but also...chagrin. Of course he wasn't squirming out of things. His sisters always said he was a man of his word. "Sure."

I needed another shower and then to stress for a good hour about what I would wear since I'd perspired all over my current clothing. I hadn't wanted to change when he'd started working and have him think I'd been ready since dawn.

"Do you want to come back and pick me up?"

"Nah." This grin was different. It was sly. Sexy. "But I do need to use your bathroom to shower. I brought a change of clothes."

"What?" Tiny sparks from neurons imploding flashed in the periphery. A naked Tate would be in my shower? Using my soap? Wiping that strong body off with *my* towels?

Not once had I considered never washing an item of clothing because a man had touched it, but I could make my bathroom a shrine to the unattainable man. The unicorn. A man who was hot, considerate, and nude in my bathroom.

His smile widened. "It's no problem, right? With the half-hour drive to my place and then back, I didn't want to waste an hour and a half of our time today."

He could go to Autumn's. She also lived on her family's land, but closer. Hell, their parents lived closer than him too.

There was no reason to say no to his request *except for self-preservation*. My decor streamed through my mind. My decorations were all well and good when I was single. But they'd been a point of contention with more than one ex who lacked a sense of humor.

He waited for my answer, but the word *yes* was stuck in my throat. "I, uh, need to get cleaned up too." As if that'd get him to offer to go to Autumn's instead.

He sobered. "You look great, Scarlett. You really do."

Uh-huh. Tate didn't have to be a player to plow through women's hearts. And I wasn't willing to cost him a few gallons of gas after he'd done hours of work for me when I had an available, albeit embarrassing, bathroom.

"Okay. Um, I need to change and wash up. Why don't I do that while you're picking up out here?"

He propped his hands on his hips and it made his chest impossibly wider. "Why doesn't it seem like you take compliments well?"

He sounded genuinely confused, and that was the only reason I didn't laugh it off. "I've been strung along by plenty of men who can talk a good game, but all they want is a woman who serves them in some way. Men will say a lot if they think it can net them sex, free housecleaning, and a lifetime cook."

He rocked back on his heels, but his gaze was thoughtful. "I was that guy once."

Shocked, I cocked my head. "Really?"

"I didn't think so. But when Tamera wasn't interested in cooking or cleaning and wanted to hire out for it all, it threw me for a loop. My mom and dad have a stereotypical traditional relationship, you know. It's what I grew up with, and I had to check my assumptions."

"And you changed?" I hung on his reply too much, but he was so open, and I didn't expect that trait from the mysterious bachelor people had been speculating about for a year.

"Somewhat. I mean, I hated having strangers in my house, but if I wasn't willing to clean it every week, I shouldn't expect her to. The cooking, well, I like cooking, but every day wasn't feasible if I was putting in twelve-hour days. Again, I couldn't expect her to come home from a work trip and get right to the kitchen." He scratched the back of his neck, deep in thought. There was more, but he didn't continue. Instead, he stroked his gaze down my body. "My compliments are sincere, Miss Scarlett."

Inside, I glowed. "I told you, Scarlett is fine."

"I like the way Miss Scarlett sounds. There's several Mr. Baileys in Bourbon Canyon between me, my dad, and my brothers, but there's only one Miss Scarlett."

"Oh." The way he said the name was nothing like my students. Theirs often had a hint of defensiveness, urgency, excitement, or just wanting my attention. Tate said Miss Scarlett like he had a secret and it was for me to uncover.

My breathing quickened, and this time, the heat swamping my body had nothing to do with the sun high overhead. "I'll let you get back to work, and I'll go wash my bits." Oh. My. God. "Clean up."

I'd officially call today How to Scare Off a Twenty-Thousand-Dollar Date.

But he didn't look mortified. His grin had layers I

was afraid to identify. Hungry. Intrigued. But also amused. "Go ahead and wash those bits, Miss Scarlett."

My face had to be the color of my name as I rushed into my house. Tate hadn't stepped inside yet, but the eight hundred square feet would shrink down to one hundred when he did. I couldn't think about that. Nor could I think about how he'd view my decorations. They'd either make him think about his grandma's house, or he'd wonder why I only had one cat when I clearly should have five.

Even if Tate Bailey saw me as more than an awkward teacher who was too broke to bid on a date with him, he'd backtrack as soon as he saw the inside of my house. Once guys got to know me, they always lost interest.

Tate

Scarlett Breen was exactly who I thought she was, yet she wasn't.

I stepped out of the shower and reread the needlepoint sign across from the toilet. An embroidered *Sit down and enjoy the show.*

Had she done the needlework?

She must have. The embroidery hanging above her coatrack read *Live, Laugh, Fuck Them All*. Done in tasteful shades of purples that made you do a double take when you read the actual message.

There was also a tongue-in-cheek framed poster of cats playing poker. The scrawl of embroidered words next to it hit me in the gut. *A Real Pussy Accepts the Odds.*

I had a feeling if I laughed, Scarlett would skitter right out of the house. She was a nervous bundle of energy. She'd answered the door this morning, and while she was much shorter than me, she'd blocked the entrance into her place.

Wash my bits.

The strict little teacher had a wacky sense of humor, and I liked it. I liked her little house too, but it was nothing like my sprawling mountain cabin. What would a meld of the two be like?

Would she make a sign for over my door? *Come and relax on my wood.*

I was getting ahead of myself. Scarlett had displayed none of the interest in me my sisters claimed she had *except for when she'd looked me over in the garage*.

I wasn't ignorant of feminine interest and I'd seen that look in women's eyes before. I liked the combination of her with that hint of desire.

I toweled off with her fluffy, summery towel. I'd only ever had solid-colored towels. Hadn't even realized they made towels with designs. Miss Scarlett lived differently than she worked, from the orange-and-purple-striped towels to the curtains that could've come from a circus tent.

My place was downright boring. Chance would get a kick out of this house, and he'd fucking love the embroidered art. Sweet, but scandalous.

I was a fan of Scarlett's pinkish-purple skirt and how it molded over her ass when she pulled weeds. And the way her light-yellow top turned her amber eyes even lighter. She wore different glasses than the black frames from yesterday. The ones she had on today were clear white with blue and peach swirls at the temples.

Dragging my mind off Scarlett's appearance so I didn't sport an erection for the second time today—the first, when her apple bottom had wiggled over the flower bed for far too long—I dug clothes out of my duffel bag and dressed. I had a clean pair of jeans, a nicer pair of black boots that I didn't use for work, and a Henley that wasn't too hot for this time of year. I pushed the sleeves half up my arms and hauled my duffel out of the bathroom.

When I'd come inside to shower, she'd been shut in what I assumed was her bedroom. The door was open now.

My pulse kicked up at the idea of finding her in her natural environment.

But she was in the kitchen, pouring two big glasses of lemonade. She had another skirt on—thank fuck. I never thought much about women's clothing until I got a green light to access what was underneath, but with Scarlett, my brain wanted to be proactive, and skirts were accessible.

She also had on a simple pink top with spaghetti straps that matched well with the colors swirling through her white skirt. The pattern was similar to the temples of her glasses. She looked both bold and whimsical.

I kept hold of my bag and propped a shoulder against the wall to watch her work. "Did you do the needlepoint yourself?"

She froze. "Uh, yes."

"I like it."

Looking over her shoulder, she blinked at me. "Really?"

"It's funny. And clever."

The corner of her mouth kicked up, and she grabbed a jar of cherries. A few drops of the juice went into each glass. Then she plopped two cherries per cup on top of the ice. "My grandma taught me how to embroider and she used to have the funniest sayings, so I've tried to put a little of her into each one."

Of course Scarlett wouldn't be whimsical for no reason. That was the practical, practiced side of her. She used the character trait as a teacher and to remember a loved one. "My grandma taught me how to judge a good bourbon when I was fourteen."

She grabbed both glasses and turned, a fond smile on her face. "Grandparents, right?"

"Exactly." I dug in my bag and brandished a half-pint of Summit Gem, our highest-quality bourbon. "I brought you some."

Her brows crept up. She set the lemonade down. "I'm not a big drinker."

"Neither am I."

More surprise crept into her face. "Don't you have to sample and stuff? I've heard your sisters talk about it."

"Yeah, that's the fun part, and we were raised learning how to describe a batch of bourbon. Oddly enough, that's why we're not big drinkers. It's an art. It's chemistry. It's a hobby. You don't want cheap shit after you've learned what goes into the best, and you don't want to overdo it and ruin your taste for a family passion." I set my bag by the wall. "However, the younger me would've had a different answer."

Her laughter shot straight into my chest. "I can picture it. I think your sisters were the same. So your parents were okay with it?"

"Mama would get so upset with them, but Grandpa

always said the business was in my bones, not alcoholism."

"Did it keep you out of the parties in the pastures?"

I grinned. "No."

She chuckled again and there was very little I wouldn't do to coax a smile from this woman. When she wasn't nervous or serious, she was radiant.

She pushed her glasses up. "Thirsty?"

"I am." A quirky, colorful little teacher was making me parched.

She sat primly at the end of the table, one foot crossed over the other and the billowy fabric of her skirt draped over her legs.

I took a seat close to her and angled to face her. I had brought water, but I chugged the lemonade. Sweetness burst over my tongue. Scarlett would taste this sweet. I smacked my lips. "That's good. Homemade?"

A smile ghosted over her lips. "Country Time. But I like to cut up lemons to put with it and then add some maraschino cherry syrup."

I plucked a cherry out and bit it off the stem. Twirling the stem, I glanced around the kitchen. "You moved here from Bozeman?"

She nodded. "I would've been fine moving back after college. My parents are there, but I wanted something different too, only not far from them."

"You're close?"

Her smile was fond. "Yes. I'm a bona fide daddy's girl. Where he went, I wanted to go. Both my parents are teachers, so..." She shrugged. "I wanted a school district big enough to have typical classrooms, but not overpopulated classrooms."

"Hard to find?"

"Yes. Most definitely. Bozeman is growing so fast."

I polished off my lemonade and rescued the last cherry. "I love the town, but it was a relief once I finally decided to move back home." I finished my cherry. She studied her glass. Was she avoiding looking at me? Was she universally shy or just around me?

Something about the challenge of getting through her shyness appealed to me. I'd been attracted to her since that first parent-teacher meeting. I'd sat, uncomfortable and shocked at the strength of my body's response, and listened to her tell me the issues with Chance. Only she hadn't made me feel like a shitty dad like other teachers had. They had assumed that, since I looked the way I did, I must be a "boys will be boys" kind of guy instead of considering what the divorce had done to my son. Ultimately, the reason Chance misbehaved was not their problem, only the outcome, but Scarlett was the first teacher who hadn't spoken as if *I* was part of the problem. She'd also complimented him on the good things he had done and spoke as if there was so much more she couldn't wait to see him do.

Chance played it off like she was annoyed, but I'd seen that little chest puff with pride.

Scarlett's frosted-sugar-cookie scent overwhelmed my senses, and the urge to nuzzle her hair struck me. I had to stick with the conversation, or I'd lose myself. It was more than my lack of a sex life. "I knew moving home was the right decision after our third meeting."

She finally looked at me. "Third?" Chewing her lower lip, her brow furrowed. My finger itched to smooth across that plump lip and make sure she didn't harm it. "That was the playground incident—where he threw snowballs at another boy?"

"Yep. You didn't act like it was the end of the world. I mean, I know he shouldn't have done it. He knows he shouldn't have done it, and he still did it."

"For a ten-year-old boy, it's normal, impulsive behavior." She lifted a shoulder. "The other boy, he loves snowball fights, but he's learned enough to know that he has to convince someone else to start them so he doesn't get in as much trouble. The new kid was the perfect target."

I knew the other kid's parents. His mom had simultaneously bitched me out and flashed me her cleavage. His dad had been pickled, probably with our family's product, so I hadn't held their son's behavior against him. That kid had an uphill battle in life. "Anyway, you didn't treat me like I was an awful parent and my kid was going to be a fuckup for life."

"That's happened before?" A cherry slipped between her ripe lips.

"Mostly after the divorce. A little before, but I guess Tamera took the brunt of it since they always called her."

"I wasn't sure what to expect out of you." The crests of her cheeks were dusted with pink. The admission was hard for her.

"Why? You thought I'd yell?"

"I don't know. I'd only heard about you from Autumn and Summer. You didn't sound scary, just very serious."

I'd had to be. I was the oldest Bailey, and my father was in a long battle with cancer. I juggled two industries between me and six other siblings. It was like herding cats some days. But in Scarlett's house, the pressure wasn't weighing on me. It couldn't when the word "pussy" was in needlepoint across from me. "Speaking of—how did you get in thick with my sisters?

Autumn, I can see. You two work together. Summer is..."

Affection blazed across her face. "Summer says and does things I wish I was brave enough to do."

"Like buying a moody bachelor for a day?"

Her smile faded, and she rolled her lips in. "I'm sorry about the trouble. I didn't know."

"We've covered that." I tapped my fingers on my glass. I couldn't push her too hard. Today wasn't easy for her. "Do you know why she did it?"

If I'd thought she'd admit to a raging secret crush on me, I was left disappointed. She grabbed my glass and brought both the empties to her sink. She dumped the ice out and whisked them into the dishwasher. "I don't. It was a complete surprise."

She claims you like me, sounded too childish. "Summer is a force, but she does what she thinks is right."

"Can't argue with the large donation to charity." Her back was to me as she wiped off the counter.

"I'm glad she did it." When Scarlett stiffened, I continued. "I wanted to get to know you more."

Again, if I'd thought she'd be thrilled that I was interested in her, I was left a wanting man.

She gave me a deadpan look. "You don't have to lay it on to make me feel better, Tate."

"I mean it."

"Mm." She wiped the counter a third time.

The back of my neck grew hot. She thought I was putting on an act?

Why wouldn't she? I'd been a mess of nerves and lust when I'd met with her at the school. I'd kept my reactions to a minimum. I'd been worried about my kid and aroused by his teacher. Hell of a predicament to be in at the elementary school I'd gone to as a kid. I'd become a one-word-response man. No wonder she thought I was faking.

I rose and plucked the rag from her hand. Yes, I was looming over her, and I meant to. "You're not my son's pretty teacher anymore."

She propped a hip against the counter and folded her arms. "Tate, really. You don't have to turn on the charm. Twenty grand is a lot of money, and it's not like I'm going to report to Wilna that the date was shitty."

Genuinely confused, I rubbed the back of my neck. My come-ons had never bounced off a wall before. "Scarlett, I'm not stringing you along."

She rolled her gaze toward me. "You're a good man. I could tell when Chance told me about the divorce and why you moved here. I know from the talk around town. And from your family. You're a responsible man. Your sisters gush about you and how well you helped care for them after they moved in with you."

I smiled, warmth infusing my chest. I thought the world of my family, and to hear they thought the same went far. But I didn't want to talk about them. "You think I'm trying to make this date a fairy tale for you?"

She nodded, open acceptance in her eyes.

That wasn't good enough. "Why don't you think I'd be interested in you?"

"I'm well over thirty, for one."

I recoiled like she'd slapped me. "Holy shit. Don't hold back."

She held up her hands. "Sorry. It's just...I listened to the gossip. I'm sorry. I don't know your life."

"I wasn't trolling college campuses asking girls if they're legal." Irritation scraped my lungs.

Was that what people said? I liked 'em young? I was forty-two, and sometimes the women I dated were significantly younger than me, but even fifteen years younger put them well beyond the college years. Hell, it put them past the graduate school years. I'd been thirty-seven when I divorced. Had people heard I'd dated a twenty-eight-year-old and thought I was perched over her cradle, ready to snatch her?

Fucking hell.

"I'm sorry." She was waving her hands, her face fire-engine red. "I'm sorry. It's none of my business, really. I'm sorry. I meant to point out that I'm approaching my midthirties. I'm a teacher—I'm not wearing power suits that show off my defined calves or making companies millions in sales."

Did she know Tamera?

"I embroider the word 'fuck,' and that's the wildest I get." She opened her mouth again and snapped it shut as if afraid to confess any more.

"I don't want power suits or parties, and I happen to think your calves are quite nice." All truth.

"Well, that's nice of you, but it's okay. I'm not the life of the party or a boss bitch and I'm okay with that."

But I was getting the impression other guys hadn't been. I'd love to throttle them. At the same time, I was glad they were epically mistaken about sweet and sexy Miss Scarlett so I could be the one with her now.

"Are you ready to eat?" she asked.

A cat sauntered out of the back bedroom, mewed, and marched right for me. I clocked her approach—and the way Scarlett jumped up to grab for the cat.

"Sorry." She lifted the cat, but the tiny feline strained for me.

"For what?"

"Lilith. She loves strangers, and the more apathetic you are toward cats, or especially if you dislike them or are allergic to them, the more she's attracted to you. I would've thought she'd learned her lesson."

"I like cats." I'd had a million barn cats that looked like Lilith.

She hugged the long-haired tabby to her chest. "She's really pushy."

I held my arms out. "Give her to me."

She clutched the cat tighter.

"Jesus, Scarlett. Who hurt the cat?"

Her expression blanched, but she petted Lilith like she had to calm the raging beast down when the cat only headbutted her and started purring. "An ex."

Hell. I'd been sarcastic, but wasn't this a revelation? The ex was the missing part of this conversation. "Is that ex the reason you won't take me seriously?"

She scratched Lilith behind the ears. Would she answer? "Tate Bailey, do you *seriously* want to date me?"

"*Seriously*, yes." And she hadn't answered my question. What ex could I hunt down and return tenfold whatever he'd done to the kitty? "Tell me about the ex."

She snuggled the contented cat. The purring got louder. "He was a shitty person, and I let him be for too long."

My sisters had fallen too often into the same cycle. "Why? Don't get me wrong, his poor behavior wasn't your fault, but you don't strike me as someone who'd put up with it."

She sighed and set Lilith down. The cat beelined for me. I would have picked her up, but Scarlett was tense, her hands twisting together as she monitored the kitty.

"It's a small town, and I get tired of embroidering alone on Friday nights."

Then I was glad my sisters had dragged her to the auction on a Friday night. "What'd he do?"

She caught herself twining her fingers together and folded them to her chest. "I could take the snide comments about my style—or lack of."

"There's nothing wrong with your style." Honestly, I hadn't noticed her appearance as much as I'd noticed *her*.

"Thanks," she mumbled. Lilith was rubbing her face against my pants leg. "Are you—is that okay?" She was primed, ready to jump to Lilith's defense.

"Can I pick her up?" Anything to put Scarlett at ease. I wasn't going to punt the kitty across the room. Scarlett didn't answer right away. "I haven't ever had an indoor cat, but I've been known to sit with the barn cats for hours to get out of work. Even as an adult—don't tell my brothers."

Finally, she relaxed. "Okay."

I lifted Lilith, and damn, if I could get Scarlett this boneless and pliant around me, it'd be a monumental achievement. I scratched the cat behind the ears, and her purr reignited.

"He was mean to her."

I wanted to growl, but I was too afraid to startle either the cat or Scarlett. "Who's the bastard who insulted you and hurt animals?"

She perched on the end of the chair she'd vacated earlier. "He moved away before you came to town. Peter Glasser. He didn't hurt her per se, but he'd put her outside and claim she'd escaped. Lilith has been a spoiled indoor cat her entire life."

"That bastard."

She nodded, her loving gaze on her cat. "He is, yes. The neighbors would help me look for her, and then Mrs. Mulberry"—she pointed to one side of her house—"saw him one day. He dumped Lilith on the edge of town by the highway."

I'd find Peter Glasser and punch him in his pussy-hating face.

"When I confronted him," she continued, "he exploded. Said he hated this town and he was sick of me. Said I bored him to death and that if he had to endure one more night of needlepoint and murder shows, he'd poke himself in the eyes with my needles and frame me for his death."

"Me and my sisters would help you hide the body." What a dickweed.

She chuckled, but it didn't erase the sadness and hurt from her face. "He said Bourbon Canyon was a good place for me. It was uneventful, predictable, and plain, just like me. And he said I'd die alone like the crazy cat lady I was destined to be."

I puffed out a breath. During the worst of our marriage, my ex and I had never been that hurtful toward each other. We were no longer in love, but we had mutual respect.

I carefully set Lilith down. She returned to rubbing against my legs. I grabbed both of Scarlett's hands in mine. "Listen. He was a complete asshole. You can't take a narcissist's opinion as fact." I rubbed my thumbs along the backs of her hands. Damn, her skin was as soft as it looked.

"Thanks. What he said has...stayed with me. Looking back, I can see the mind games he played the two years we were together, but for those two years, I didn't notice."

And his words had done damage.

That fucker.

"I think it's because it was nothing new." She ran her lower lip through her teeth. "I've heard it before from other guys I've dated, just not so vehemently."

Fuck them all. "Can I take you out because I want to?"

Her muscles flexed under my hands. A flinch. Was she reminding herself I was paid to be here? "Sure. Let's get some food."

Fuck.

I loved my sisters, but I was also upset with them. They couldn't have known it, but Summer and Autumn buying me for Scarlett was a harsh dent to her confidence, one I might not be able to smooth.

Scarlett

The stares from everyone were a million spiders crawling up my back and into my hair. The whole town knew this date was part of the auction.

I should've gone to his house. This was ridiculous. We were a spectacle.

The manager of Canyon Grill, Curly Binstock, bustled out of the kitchen when we arrived and seated us, gushing over the mountain view, as if I didn't eat here regularly when even embroidery on Friday nights got to me. Summer, Autumn, and I would meet at Curly's for our girls' night, and the manager hadn't made an appearance any of those times. Not even when Wynter or June were in town and would join us.

I pushed my lettuce around my plate. After the humiliating confession in my house, I had the constant urge to flee. Seeing him with my cat would make any ghosting after this date worse.

Lilith had liked Peter too—for the first year. Then, when she'd started getting "lost," I should've realized that she would hide when he was around. Instead of sleeping on the bed, she'd be under it. When he walked into the kitchen, she'd sneak around the edges of the room, then dash under the bed.

Humiliation flamed my cheeks. The blush had almost died down, and then we'd walked into the restaurant and had become a show. Stares. Murmurs. We'd been seated for twenty minutes, and their gawking crawled over my skin.

How much of what Peter had said about me being a dud had gotten around town? Were people making bets over when Tate would run, not walk, away from this date?

Tate took a drink. He'd just gotten water. Not what I expected after Curly had gushed about the various lines of Copper Summit liquor they carried.

He carefully set his glass down, his gaze on me as I tried to admire the mountains and take my mind off the other patrons. "Do you want to leave?"

"No, it's fine."

It was foolish. No one knew what Peter had said when we'd broken up. Or did they? How much had Peter told others during the two years we were together? I had begun to question it all. Some of my kids' parents knew I was into needlework, those who had also been customers of Peter's at the implement dealer. I thought it'd been small talk. But had he complained about how boring and predictable I was too? How I was assigned the kids who were more of a handful because my sedate personality could put anyone to sleep?

"Scarlett." He pushed away his empty soup bowl.

He'd had an entire bowl of chicken tortilla soup and hadn't spilled one drop on himself. The guy was unreal. Half the time, I wondered if my boobs were a special magnet for food.

"Tate, it's fine."

"It's not. You don't like being the center of attention, and we were literally put in the center for the attention."

I grimaced and glanced around. Tables surrounded us. Booths lined the windows. The most private booth in the back corner by the bathrooms was empty. "Yes, we were."

"Curly always likes it when the Baileys dine here."

"'Baileys' being the critical part."

His gaze sharpened. "What do you mean?"

Dammit. I didn't want to spend the whole day complaining about the various attitudes in town. "Your sisters don't impress him as much."

The Baileys had taken in Summer, Autumn, and their other two sisters as fosters and then adopted them. The girls had kept their last name of Kerrigan. Darin and Mae Bailey had wanted them to feel like they would always have a part of their parents with them. Most folks in town lumped them in with "the Baileys." But others, like Curly, thought it was like a partial rejection, a way to say, *but these aren't ours*.

Displeasure rippled across Tate's face.

I didn't know Mae and Darin that well, but from what I'd heard, they were welcoming and supportive. They loved their three boys, they'd fostered several kids over the years, and they'd adopted the four little girls who'd lost their parents in a ravine when they'd been out camping.

Tate's lips were in a flat line. "If only he knew the

reason he gets a deal on Copper Summit products is because of Summer and how much she loves this damn town."

"She does remind him periodically, don't worry."

He laughed, garnering more attention, but when his smile was aimed my way, I preened.

I was the one who'd made him laugh. He stalked through town like he was a brooding mountain man, and how wrong had that impression been? He was congenial and, at times, even jovial.

Of course, he'd been a salesman for years. He'd run the Bozeman offices and arranged deals that had put the Baileys at the top of their industry.

"Let's have them pack our food to go. We can picnic somewhere."

A picnic. It wouldn't be his place. Disappointment flowed through my veins. I could've been in his house. I might appreciate being protected from possible rejection, but the regret was growing too large to care right now.

"That sounds nice." Thankfully I'd gotten beef tips and didn't have to worry about how to saw a steak with plastic flatware.

Fifteen minutes later, we were sitting on a picnic bench in the park outside of town. The picnic area was several yards above the water. It was June, and the waterline was high this time of year with the mountain runoff. The rush of the river mingled with the bugs and birds.

"It's gorgeous out." The wind ruffled my hair, but I was riveted to him. Eating out of a foam container shouldn't be so sexy. He'd talked the chef into chopping his steak. This was the fanciest meal I'd ever had outside.

"This is my second favorite fishing spot." He dug a bun out of the to-go bag and handed it to me.

I accepted it. He must have scammed more buns out of Curly too. "I've heard there's good fishing here. What's your top fishing spot, or is it a secret?"

His grin was quick. "A lake near my house. I used to spend so much time there with my brothers. It was a place we could get away from the girls and any other annoying kids that were living with us at the time."

"Was that hard? Going from a family with three kids to seven and sometimes more?"

He nodded but couldn't hide the guilt. "It was. To go from the three of us to the four girls was an adjustment, but then Mom and Dad kept accepting fosters. As an adult, I can admire what they did and how they tried to help."

"But as a kid?"

"Everyone in your business? Having to share all your shit? It sucked. But then I'd feel bad. Some of them would come to our place with nothing."

"That's awful. I don't know the homelife of my students, but a lot of times, I can guess."

"What did you think of Chance's homelife?" He grinned as he speared a piece of steak. "Truthfully now. I won't get offended."

I almost didn't play along, but it wasn't like I had anything bad to say. "Well, I was already friends with Autumn and Summer. They said you were a corporate big shot."

He groaned. "They do not describe me like that."

"It wasn't accurate?"

"I didn't wear suits," he grumbled, and it was adorable. The big bearded guy was offended that I might think he was a paper pusher. "Unless I had to. It's a distillery, but when you're asking someone to spend millions on your product, you wear a damn tie."

"They painted a stern picture of you. So, I thought you ran a tight ship at home. Then I met Chance, and I had to decide if it was such a tight ship he acted out when the restraints were loosened at school, or was it a normal home, but he felt like he was missing something."

"You think he feels that?"

"He misses his mom," I said softly, but only because Tate knew that already. He'd alluded to it at our meetings.

"He does. She calls a couple times a week. And she'll be in Bozeman a few weeks before the end of summer. He'll stay with her then. She can handle two weeks."

Was he trying to convince himself? "That'll be good for him, but I imagine you'll see some regression in his behavior."

"Thanks for the warning."

I ripped a chunk off the bun. "For what it's worth, you and your ex are doing really well."

He impaled another piece of meat, a line running across his brow. "Oh yeah?"

My fingers itched to push a lock of hair off his head and smooth the line away. "Yeah. Trust me. I see the fallout of bad divorces a lot more than I care to."

He sat back and thought for a moment. "Thanks. I know we did the right thing for us, but I always wondered if it was the right thing for him."

"He's a good kid."

"You saw that when others didn't."

His compliment ignited a spark deep inside me, stronger than any other nice thing he could say. I took my job seriously. Yes, the extra outside of class could wear on a person, and yes, the pay wasn't as much as a lot of professions, but I really liked making a difference—standardized testing and regulations be damned. "Thank you."

"Huh. That's the way to get to you—complimenting your job?" I sputtered, but he pointed his fork at me. "You, Miss Scarlett, almost had me shaking in my boots during our first meeting."

"I did not."

"Believe it. Then your tits took the rest of my attention."

My startled laughter rang out, scaring a bird from a nearby tree. "They did not."

His gaze dropped to my chest. "You sure about that, teach?"

My nipples turned instantly hard. Throbbing in a way they never had before. Tate just happened to reference them, and they came alive. "Tate," I warned. I couldn't survive his flirting and then be happy with a murder show by myself.

"You're a sexy woman, Miss Scarlett. It's not my fault if you don't know it, but now that I see you're horrifically ignorant, I'm duty bound to show you."

"Show?" My throat closed up on the word.

Pink touched his cheeks. "I meant tell, but I'm more than happy to show you."

Oh god. I'd read too much into it. I'd embarrassed Tate Bailey. He'd stood unflinching while a church full of women haggled over him, even when his sister won the bid. He hadn't meant "show me" *literally*, yet I'd jumped on it and humiliated myself. I stuffed a beef tip in my mouth, keeping my gaze planted on the peeling paint of the picnic table.

"What's going on in that sharp, overanalyzing mind of yours?"

"Nothing," I said around my mouthful.

"Scarlett." He set his utensils down. "Did I go too far?"

Not far enough. "I'm fine. My food's getting cold, and it's getting late." No, it wasn't. But I was ready to crawl under my blanket with the AC on full blast and learn about a horrific murder until I remembered I couldn't die of unrequited sexual need.

Tate

Figuring this woman out shouldn't be so hard. She spoke freely about her impressions of me. She didn't shy away or change the subject when I brought up my sisters and the kids my family fostered. Brushing against the topic was enough to stop a lot of people midsentence who'd find somewhere else to be.

Everyone knew the tragic story of my sisters' parents. They talked about the accident enough behind my back but to my face? No.

Scarlett could tackle the hard subjects, but she didn't realize the hardest subject was her.

Fuck that ex of hers.

I bet men like him were drawn to her. Before that

bastard, other guys had probably used her to make themselves feel better too. And once she refused to cave to their man-child ways, they'd likely jetted and blamed her.

And deep down, she believed the crap they'd spewed.

We finished our meal, chatting about the water, the type of fish I'd caught in the river and the weather. She mentioned fishing and camping with her parents. She left unsaid that her exes hadn't liked either activity, and she hadn't done much as an adult.

I could change that if she let me.

Throughout the whole meal, I thought about how I could show her how amazing her tits were. I hadn't wanted to be too forward, but she'd shut down right after.

Did she want me to show her?

She never said she didn't like me. She only said she didn't believe I was into her. She never said she didn't want to date me—only that she was sorry my sisters had intervened against our will.

The truth was in everything she didn't say.

So I'd have to keep trying to win her over.

"Want to go for a walk with me?" I asked as we cleaned up our trash and stuffed the garbage into the supposedly bear-proof trash bin.

She brushed her hands off, frowning. "I've sweated enough around you already."

"Ah, honey, not nearly enough." Damn, I couldn't help but push it.

Her cheeks turned into an instant flame, and she pushed her glasses up. "I should get home."

I'd give her this reprieve, but I wasn't done trying.

The space she so desperately wanted lasted only until

we crowded into my pickup and I was surrounded by her frosted-cookie scent. I propped an elbow on the middle console, wishing I had my truck from high school with its solid bench seat. Then I could have slid her right next to me. "Scarlett, do you trust me?"

"About what?"

Of course she wouldn't say yes. Not Miss Scarlett. "I want you to believe me."

"Tate." Regret hung in her voice. I didn't like it.

I cupped her chin between my thumb and forefinger. Her eyes widened, and I slowly leaned in. "I want you to believe me, and I'd like to show you."

Gently, I touched my lips to hers. When she didn't pull back or haul off and punch me, I added pressure.

Still, she didn't squirm away. I flattened my hand along her jaw and cupped it around the back of her neck. I twisted my torso, careful to keep from separating us, and embraced her as best I could with a console in the way.

A tiny whimper sounded in her throat.

I gave her an answering growl and stroked my tongue into her mouth. She tasted exquisite. I'd expected sweet, but we'd just finished a savory meal, and I could gobble her up.

My erection raged, and I was helpless to hold it back while I was touching her. Only my position kept it tucked safely but torturously in my jeans.

Tentatively, her tongue met mine.

Yes.

Stroke for stroke, she met me, growing bolder, needier.

Fuck yes.

I was ready to climb over the hard plastic between us when tires spun out on gravel outside the pickup.

She pulled back with a gasp. A carload of teens skidded to a stop next to us. A young girl with large sunglasses and wild blond hair hung out the passenger window. "Way to go, Miss Scarlett!"

She'd yelled so loud we didn't need the window open, but Scarlett lowered it anyway. "Good evening, Brandy," she said calmly.

The guy behind the wheel grinned in a way that made me want to peel his lips off his face. "How much did that kiss cost?"

Scarlett stiffened. "That's rude, Jacob."

He laughed obnoxiously. "Yeah, but you can't send me to the principal's office this time."

That little shit. "Listen, kid." I gave him my best *cross to the other side of the street* glare. "If you're not eighteen yet, I can have this little chat with your dad, and if that prick ain't in the picture, I'll be glad to tell Officer Tom you're harassing my date."

He paled, but his smug grin stayed in place. "My mom said she got with you when you were free."

Son of a bitch. I'd dated this kid's mom? From what Jacob said, I'd done more with her.

"Jacob," Scarlett said in her stern teacher tone. "Some women learn their worth a lot later in life. Brandy, I'm hoping you learn it a lot faster than some."

"Have you learned it yet?" Brandy asked, saccharine sweet, her pointed gaze shifting to me.

Scarlett's inhale was deep. I wished I could see her face, but her back was ramrod straight. "Yes, actually. I have two awesome friends who were willing to pay twenty grand for me to go on a date with the best man they know, a man who no longer freely gives himself or his time away. I highly recommend good friends and good men. Ten out of ten." She waggled her fingers as she rolled the window up.

I was staring at her when she turned, grabbed my face, and hauled me toward her.

Scarlett

What was I doing?

All the best things.

I was scaling this bearded mountain man like he was a cliff face and I was a free climber.

I hip-checked my front door open, my lips plastered to his, my tongue down his throat. I tossed the keys somewhere inside and kicked the door closed as he wedged us farther in. He lifted me, and I wound my arms and legs around him.

"Scarlett," he said against my mouth, then kissed a path to my ear.

Oh my god, that shouldn't feel so damn good. Shivers traced down my back. "Yeah?" I didn't recognize myself. I'd managed to give out proper adult advice and totally diss an asshole nineteen-year-old who'd given me heartburn the entire year he was in my class. To top it off, I'd smacked down my guards and indulged with Tate.

"I need to get inside of you." He was at my throat now, his mouth hot, his tongue licking circles. I was still tied around him, my hands hooked behind his neck and my ankles crossed around his hips.

"Okay."

He jerked his head up to peer into my eyes. "You sure?"

If there was one thing I was sure about, it was that I wanted to have sex with the scowling dad of one of my former students. If he was willing, I wasn't going to look much deeper. I wouldn't do that to myself. This was for me.

"You remember the fourth time I asked you to come to my class for a meeting?"

He nodded and kneaded my ass as he held me against him.

"I didn't have to. It was nothing that couldn't have gone home in a letter."

A slow, sexy grin spread across his face. "Why, Miss Scarlett, I'd like to finally show you how obsessed with those tits of yours I've been."

"You really— My boobs?" I hated being this insecure girl. I was with a strong, confident man from a formidable family who'd single-handedly saved this town with their business and then gone on to save kids. And here I was, having anxiety about my body.

"Yours." He curled his fingers under the hem of my shirt. "I look at them and think they'll fit perfectly in my hands. I think that your nipples will be tight little pebbles in my mouth, and I think you'll quiver when I run my tongue over them."

I was already trembling. "Tate. I want to find out if you're right."

"Lift your arms, Scarlett."

I did as he demanded. How could I not?

The shirt went over my head and onto the living room floor. We hadn't even moved beyond the entry nook.

He was about to move farther into the house, but I gasped. "My blinds are open."

"Here works just fine." He helped untwine my legs, so I didn't tip out of his hold.

He put space between us and stopped, his gaze riveted on my bra. Oh no. I'd forgotten I'd changed out of my polka dot set when I cleaned up after the yard work.

"Pink smiley faces, Scarlett?"

"I like, uh, fun undergarments." This was it. The end of the best make-out session I'd ever had. I wanted this so bad, and my fun undies had been a point of contention before.

Your idea of lingerie is a libido killer. Peter had been awful to me and my cat.

A brow ticked up, heavy interest infusing his brown irises. "Are all of them fun?"

"A lot. I have plain white too." How sexy did I sound? I could embroider that for my underwear drawer. *I have plain white too*. Ugh.

"Every day, Miss Scarlett. Every day, I want to know what you have on underneath your clothing." Before I could hook my hopes on that *every day*, he reached behind me. A deft snap and my bra was falling from my shoulders.

A groan eked out of him as he palmed both breasts. "Perfect," he muttered, and I believed him.

He meant it. My pink smiley faces weren't a turnoff,

but then Tate was a level of man my ex could never attain.

Each stroke of his calloused fingertips sent ripples of pleasure over my skin. I'd never been so sensitive. And when he bent to do exactly what he'd described and tongued my nipples, a shiver racked my body.

A low chuckle reverberated through him and into me. "Knew it. You're so damn responsive."

Then he dropped to his knees. My breath caught. Without him blocking me, I was suddenly exposed in the privacy of my home. I stuffed my hands into his hair. "Tate?"

His fingers skated up my calves. "You with me?"

"I don't know," I answered honestly.

"How 'bout you focus on me and what I'm doing to you and quit worrying about the rest." He wasn't asking.

He didn't even know what the rest was. I didn't either. I had my suspicions. Past disappointments. Past insults. Past shitty men.

So far, Tate hadn't ticked any of those boxes. He'd been kind and helpful. Charming and sensual. Now he was intoxicating and passionate. I wasn't used to those last two centered on me. But Tate was all of them, and he directed them at me.

Me.

The back of my head thunked the wall. "Okay."

I closed my eyes, let my boobs hang out, and enjoyed the way he swept the fabric of my skirt up.

"I'm dying to know if you wore a matching set."

I opened my eyes and met his gaze, acutely grateful I paired my fun undergarments together. He slipped his hands higher under my skirt. The warm tips hit the hem of my underwear and I trembled. Residual anxiety spread through me, and I fought not to push him away.

He disappeared under the colorful drape of my skirt. A long growl had me clutching the wall behind me.

"I'm going to get an erection the next time I see a pink smiley face." He tugged my underwear down, and his hot breath wafted over my feverish skin.

The panties fell to the floor, and he carefully lifted my foot to free them and toss them in the direction of my bra and shirt. Then his hands were back at my inner thighs, coaxing them apart.

"Let me in, Scarlett. I need to see how wet you are for me."

I had to squeeze my eyelids closed again. He was too much. This shouldn't be out of my comfort zone, but a rejection from Tate carried more significance, and I hadn't known him as long as the others I'd been with.

I bit my lip before I explained that I didn't keep up on personal landscaping. I was single. I'd had zero dating prospects before Summer intervened, and I certainly hadn't thought tonight would end up with his head at my crotch and his fingers getting closer to the fiery inferno that had become my center.

Fuck it. I lifted a leg, and he smoothly propped my foot on his shoulder. My whole body jolted when his tongue plowed through my folds and went to my clit like he had a private GPS.

"Oh god, Tate."

"Get nice and loud, honey."

I melted against his mouth, against his body. Only his hands holding me open kept me rooted in place. The leg that was on the floor vibrated as he licked across my clit. He tested different speeds and pressures, but I was a lousy pupil. I didn't know what I liked other than him to continue doing what he was doing. It didn't matter what he did with his tongue, I kept coiling tighter and tighter, energy compressing for an impending explosion.

He hooked a hand around the outside of my thigh and settled in. Complete dedication.

Everything inside me ruptured, and pleasure infused every cell. "Tate! Oh god! Tate!"

I shook so much I had no idea how he could hold me up, but he kept going until I had nothing left. My foot started sliding off his shoulder. Only his face was holding me up now. I'd smother him. I'd end him. And then I'd have to explain to the town how I'd killed their adored bachelor with the orgasm he'd given me. But he anchored me in place.

Awareness came back as he pulled away and pressed a soft kiss to my inner thigh. "That was glorious, Miss Scarlett." He dragged the skirt off his head. His hair was mussed and his beard glistened with...me. "Now it's time to see you shatter when I'm inside you."

"Again?" I'd orgasmed twice in one night before, but it'd been like a flooded engine trying to turn over. With a ton of concentration and sweat, eventually, I'd gotten there. This climax had been the strongest one ever. He expected me to do it again?

"Again," he confirmed, rising. "I've been dreaming of getting under this teasing skirt all night. I'm going to fuck you in it. Then I'm going to strip it off and fuck you again."

Two times? "I guess that'd make us even on the orgasm side," I mumbled as he took out his wallet, withdrew a condom, and tossed his wallet on the floor with the rest of my stuff.

I was down to one article of clothing, and he'd shed only his wallet. Yet, coming until I screamed had robbed me of my earlier self-consciousness.

"Two for me. Three for you." He ripped open the packet with his teeth and yanked his zipper down.

I could have contributed more to the undressing of him, but I was stuck on his words. "You think you're going to make me come three times?"

"I know it." He had his erection out and rolled on the condom.

Holy crap. His cock was out, and I was getting my own private show. My brain slowed down, focusing on his girth and the veins that lined him from tip to base. I wouldn't be coherent after he was done with me.

He shoved his shirt out of the way, but it continued to fall over his thick cock. With a growl, he ripped his shirt off.

I was dreaming. He wasn't real. His chest was a work of art. Were pecs supposed to look that hard? I flattened my palms on them. Warm and hard. Not a mirage.

"Later," he said gruffly and lifted me. "I need to be in you."

I automatically wrapped my legs around him and pulled my skirt out of the way. He positioned himself at my entrance, and we both looked down. My wet, swollen flesh surrounded the thick tip of him. Another private show, one I honestly had never watched before. He was rapt, rocking his hips to wet the broad tip. Then he slowly pushed inside, filling me as inch after inch disappeared.

A moan slipped out of me. I wasn't this noisy girl during sex. I wasn't a shouter. I didn't cry out.

I, apparently, had been with all the wrong partners.

Until a bourbon bachelor had convinced me to go on a twenty-thousand-dollar date with him.

He eased out and pushed back in, tipping his forehead to mine. "You feel like heaven, do you know that? You're so fucking hot and wet, and I can't get enough, but I can barely last longer than two strokes."

He was lying. I didn't know what number stroke he was on, but my body was tracking each move, ratcheting higher toward another crest. And he was right there with me, taut except for the expert swing of his hips.

No fast, frantic fucking for Tate Bailey. He held my legs apart and plundered me. I twined my fingers into his hair and moved as much as I could with him.

"You're coming again." He kissed my cheek and worked his way down my neck. The silky roughness of his beard ignited my nerve endings, turning them into tiny fireworks.

"Oh" was all I could say. Then, another "*Oh*" when he hit the best spot deep inside me.

A small chuckle left him and he continued teasing my neck with his facial hair, but when he slid his fingers between us to rest on my clit, I realized he was playing me. He was the master of my body, and he knew exactly what to do.

I didn't mind. With this, I trusted him.

Sensation from my neck to my clit bloomed. I didn't know where my peak was until I rammed into it.

No coherent word left my mouth. I just cried out, long and loud. The second climax was more intense than the first. His hot tongue was at my neck, his hard cock pumping in and out, and his finger on my clit drew it all together into one blinding orgasm.

I was distantly aware of him climaxing with me, his

strokes shortening, and my name grunted from his mouth.

Before I started my tumble down, I was aware of two things. I'd managed to keep my glasses on through all this. And Tate Bailey had ruined me for all other men.

Tate

I woke up with a warm body snuggled into me for the first time in months. Over a year?

Hell, after the divorce, I didn't have sleepovers. I had a sitter who was usually a sibling, and they would have given me endless shit about overnights. Then Chance would hear and start asking about the complexities of stepmoms. As a result, I kept my dates limited to a few hours only. If we could fuck in that time, fine. If not, I had a career to keep afloat and a son to care for.

I rubbed my eyes. A warm lump at my feet made a trilling sound. A head full of messy hair lifted from my shoulder and blinked at me. Lilith was on my legs, and Scarlett was tucked into my side. She was as beautiful in the morning as she was every other part of the day.

A slow, sultry smile spread across those lips I wanted to nibble on. I could spend the whole morning— *Fuck*. Chance.

I scrambled for the end table, knocking over a framed something. The cat made a disgruntled noise and jumped off the bed. Scarlett got dislodged in my rush.

"What time is it?"

The play of emotions across her face explained in vivid detail how I'd said the wrong thing.

Shit, I was messing this up too. "Chance is at my parents'. I told him I'd pick him up by ten so we can go fishing today."

She blinked back the hurt and the *I knew it* expression. A flimsy and neutral expression in its place. She sat up and pushed her hair off her face. "Um." The blanket started falling, and she jerked it up. It should be a felony to cover those creamy breasts of hers, especially when I'd left a couple of love marks on them. "My phone is in the living room."

Where I'd tugged her skirt off after our first time. All her clothing was out there.

She hugged the blankets to her chest, and as much as I wanted to reassure her that I wasn't loving and leaving her, that I hadn't done this to make sure she got her money's worth, I had to know how badly I'd slept in. Chance had been complaining about how little we did together, and I'd told him we'd moved here so we could hang out more. If I had stayed in Bozeman, I'd have kept getting rooked back into work.

I rolled up, not caring if any blankets stayed on me. "Let me get my phone. Then we'll talk, okay?"

She glanced over her shoulder, her face half-masked by a mess of golden-brown hair, and nodded.

"I'm not ditching you." I got up and searched the floor. Had my pants made it this far? "But I promised him we'd have most of the day together." There. My jeans were peeking out from the hallway.

"You don't want to disappoint him." She dragged the blanket off and wrapped it around her shoulders, concealing everything. Next, she put her glasses on.

She wasn't being flippant. She was the type to put Chance first too, but she was also the type to convince herself I was leaving her with no plans to come back.

I would return, and it wouldn't just be for the best sex of my life. It'd be for more glimpses of the strong and quirky personality she'd shown me yesterday. It'd be to find out what embroidery project she was working on next. It'd be to take her on more picnics, or to brave Curly's with me again, or to watch her ass while she pulled weeds.

I finished dragging on my pants. My shirt. Damn, it was in the living room. I rushed down the hall. In the kitchen, the time read 10:10. *Fuck*. When had I last slept in like this?

When had I last fucked all night until I literally couldn't get it up anymore, then dived between sweet legs and gotten her off one last time?

Never. I'd never satiated myself that thoroughly before, but then, I hadn't been with Scarlett Breen before.

I gathered all our clothes and brought them to the back bedroom. She was already in loose shorts and a sleep shirt, thin enough to see the plain white bra underneath.

I didn't care. Her tits still looked amazing. I sorted her clothing onto the bed and shrugged into my shirt. "I'm late, but I want to see you again."

Her smile was placating. "Sure."

"I'm serious, Scarlett." I waggled a finger between us. "This isn't something I'm walking away from, but my son is important, and after what he went through with his mom and my work hours, I can't let him down."

Her features softened. "I understand. I really do. Go. You're late."

A buzzing came from my back pocket. I pulled out my phone. "Goddammit." I had three missed calls from my parents. "I've gotta—"

A sadness I didn't like crept into her smile. "Go, Tate. He needs you."

"I'll call you."

"Sure."

That fucking word. I'd never hated it before, and now I did. With a passion. "Scarlett—"

She held up a hand. "We can talk all we want about us, but the fact is your son comes first. We both know that if you're being genuine and you want to see me again, you'll have to talk to Chance first. I'm not willing to sneak around—this town is too small. There's already going to be talk about what happened at the park. So you need to spend time with your son, but you'll also have to decide just how much of this"—she gestured between us—"you really want because you'll have to okay it with him. You'll want his approval before you do anything."

The realism I had admired about her when we'd talked at school meetings was biting me in the ass. "I'll talk to him."

The corner of her mouth lifted. "Enjoy your fishing date."

"I'll call." Urgency moved my feet. I was late for my son, and I had promised I wasn't going to be that guy anymore.

As I got into my pickup, I waved at Mrs. Mulberry. She was shading her eyes, watching my hasty departure from her neighbor's house. Fuck, this looked bad to everyone.

I was confident about wanting to continue seeing Scarlett. We had too much burning between us, and we'd only been out together for a day. But what she'd said before I'd left was the clincher. I had promised to do better for Chance, and if he wasn't on board with a long-term girlfriend, I'd do what he asked. He had to be my first priority.

Scarlett

Three hours after Tate left, Summer pounded on my door. "I know you're in there. I have to head back to Bozeman soon, so you have to open the door."

Couldn't I get half a day to wallow in my sadness? To stop my spinning brain and tamp down the hope that Tate was serious about talking to Chance? To end the replay of Chance and I struggling for much of the year until coming to an understanding?

Chance would tell his dad an emphatic no. He didn't want a stepmom, and he definitely didn't want it to be his fourth-grade teacher.

I pushed up from my couch. Lilith made a complaining noise, but she jumped down. Twice in one day, she'd been disrupted from her sleep, and she would hold it against me.

Technically, it'd been Tate who'd woken her up this

morning. I was shocked she'd slept on his feet. The most unpredictable body part on a stranger she'd just met.

Wasn't I the same with him?

I opened the door. Summer narrowed her eyes and looked me up and down. She tapped her wedge-heeled foot and scrutinized my haphazard look, so at odds with her and her sister in their simple summer dresses.

Autumn waved from behind, an apologetic smile in place. Her auburn hair was in a braid like Summer's. "I told her to wait, but she insisted that since she was leaving today, she got to butt into your business."

Summer was unrepentant. "Blame Wynter. She's already calling me for the details. *Calling*, Scarlett. She hates talking on the phone, but she's calling before she even ignores three of my texts." She pushed past me into the living room and flopped on the floral glider rocker I had kept from my grandma's things when she'd passed.

"June's not leaving us alone either." Autumn entered, but she went to the kitchen. The fridge door squeaked open. "Ooh, you made lemonade."

"Come in," I said, closing the front door. I had hoped to polish off the lemonade for breakfast with Tate. It'd been a frivolous thought as I passed out in his arms, exhausted and sated in a way I hadn't known was possible. But no. My lemonade would have to remain a treat for my friends and my students.

Summer sat up and planted her hands on her knees. "Was the date that bad? Was he an ass? I didn't think he would be, dammit. Was I wrong? Was he—"

"No." I rubbed my temples. A dull headache was starting, and I hadn't had anything to drink. Maybe I should add the bourbon he'd given me to my glass of lemonade. "No, he was great. But you know how these things go."

Autumn appeared in the opening between the living room and kitchen. She and Summer stared at me for several moments before Summer said, "No. We don't. How did things go?"

I wasn't going to tell them I'd ridden their brother for hours. I wouldn't tell Tate's sisters that he was the best I'd ever had and I'd never find another guy to match. I wouldn't tell them I'd gotten the appeal of sex before, but it'd sort of been out of my reach—until Tate. Not only did I get the appeal, but I could become an aficionado. Dedicate my life to the study of sex with Tate.

"He mowed the lawn." In a fancy diagonal pattern I could never match. "And fixed the roof."

"He did *work*?" Autumn said flatly, disappointment rising in her gaze. "That's all?"

"No, we went out. Everyone at the grill was staring, so we got the food to go and turned it into a picnic."

Summer clapped her hands together, grinning. "So romantic."

I wasn't looking forward to the next part, but the teenagers who saw us probably weren't going to be quiet about it. "We, uh, kissed, and Jacob and Brandy caught us." Autumn would know who they were. Summer might not know the kids.

"Ooh—scandalous." Autumn exchanged a delighted look with Summer. "I think Jacob's mom and Tate had a thing in high school that went out faster than a solar-powered flashlight after sunset."

"Oh, Jacob mentioned it."

They waited. I threw my weight into my resolve. No talking about sex with Tate.

"Aaaannnd?" Summer waved her hand for me to keep going. When I didn't say anything, she crossed her arms. "Mrs. Mulberry caught me at the grocery store. I know he stayed over."

She was grinning, but tears pricked my eyes. Their thrill morphed into horror.

Summer jumped up. "Oh no, honey. What did he do?" She and Autumn swarmed me.

Tears flowed, and I couldn't stop them. "Nothing. He was more perfect than I imagined. But he overslept and kept Chance waiting, and it's all going to be up to his son, and that's what I get for being a strict teacher. Chance is never going to let his dad date me—*if* his dad even wants to date me."

Summer's hug almost cut off my air supply. She was small but strong. "Okay, the Chance part, I get. He's a kid, and he's had some changes in his life. But listen, Tate doesn't just sleep over at someone's house. Believe me, I've offered to stay at his place so he can meet another woman for more than— Anyway, he never took me up on it. He's into you—and I wouldn't have bid on him for you if I'd thought you two weren't hot for each other and wouldn't work together."

Their hold eased, and I brushed the moisture from my eyes. "Really?"

Autumn patted my shoulder, concern heavy in her gaze. "I went along with it because I hoped my brother could undo what that cocksucker Peter did to you. You're a catch and a decent guy would know it. Tate knows it."

"His kid hates me." I sniffled.

"He doesn't." Summer's smile was kind, but there was no certainty in her eyes. "He's a confused kid. There have been a lot of changes in his life, but both Tate and I will tell you that you were a good one for Chance."

A firm teacher with high expectations wasn't something a now-eleven-year-old always appreciated.

"What did Tate say?" Autumn asked.

"He said he'd call me."

And that was that. I wasn't waiting around. I'd dated guys with no kids, and they'd moved on for a lot less.

Tate

Chance had been quiet when I first picked him up. Instead of profusely apologizing, I'd told him I was sorry. I had slept in, and I hadn't meant to, and it wasn't his fault. He'd shrugged, and we had run home to grab our tackle boxes, poles, and camp chairs.

I dug in the cooler for another sparkling water. "Want a juice, bud?"

"Sure." The end of his pole dipped, and he gasped. I was poised to help him, but he reeled in a few feet of line and nothing. "Aw hell."

Fishing rule—mild swearing was allowed. The bigger the fish that got away, the stronger the swear word that could be used.

"The next one will be the real thing." I sat back down and checked my line. I hadn't cast more than three times during the time we'd been out here. The lake was quiet today, a hidden gem on Bailey land. Some days, the fish were biting, and others, they were quiet. I was only interested in the one who felt like she was getting away.

"We're getting a boat this summer, right?"

Last year, we'd brainstormed all the fun things we could do this summer. I was still settling into helping Dad with the ranch.

"That's the plan. A little fishing boat for the two of us." I'd cruised through the sales ads, but I hadn't found one I liked. I could afford to buy a brand-new one, but Dad had raised a more practical man.

Usually, when we fished, I'd go through the online ads again, but I couldn't concentrate. I hadn't let Scarlett down, other than being a shitty planner and not setting an alarm. I would call her again. But I couldn't escape the feeling that I had disappointed her.

I wouldn't know until I talked to Chance. I cleared my throat. "Hey, buddy. What if that fishing boat could hold three people?"

His face lit up. "We can bring Grandpa."

If I hadn't been in a downer of a mood before, that did it. My dad wasn't getting better. He was growing weaker and leaving home less often. I'd moved back in the nick of time. "We'll have to see how he feels. But, uh, what if...I started seeing someone?"

Chance swung his head around. His big brown eyes were shrewd. "You're dating?"

"Sort of. I went on a date last night."

"That's why you were late," he said flatly.

"Yes. I didn't think I needed to set an alarm. That was my mistake."

He fiddled with his rod and eyed his red-and-white bobber in the water. "Who were you with?"

"That's what I want to talk to you about. Because I'd like to see her again."

He kept watching the water.

"Scarlett Breen."

He recoiled. "Miss Scarlett?" His horrified astonishment wasn't heartening. "You had a sleepover with *Miss Scarlett?*"

"Yes." I schooled my expression to make it seem like a sleepover was nothing but movies and popcorn until too late at night.

His back was telephone-pole straight, his expression disgusted. "Miss Scarlett." He shook his head. "Why?"

"I really like her, and I enjoyed being with her."

"I don't like her."

This wasn't going as well as I'd hoped. "She, uh, she likes you."

He rolled his gaze toward me. At times, he could be so grown up. "She doesn't."

"She does. Her work is being a teacher; it's not her." When he didn't say anything, I kept pressing. "Chance, what do you say? I'd like to keep seeing her, but I know it'd be an adjustment after how things have been."

His thin lips flattened. "You said when we moved, it'd be just me and you."

"It is. No matter what, it'll be you and me, but we can also widen our life to include others. Like we have since we moved. Grandma and Grandpa. You see Aunt Autumn more. Uncle Tenor."

"Uncle Teller too," he added reluctantly.

"And Aunt Wynter and Aunt Junie." We only saw them more because they came to visit our parents, but I'd take any advantage I could. "Look, me working too much didn't have to do with another person. It was a balance problem. Now that I'm aware of it, I'll make sure not to act like I did before."

"You were an hour late this morning."

Forty-five minutes. My parents didn't live as far out as I did. But to Chance, those extra minutes were an eternity. "That was on me, bud. It wasn't her fault."

He thought for a moment. "I want it to be just you and me."

That was that.

His bobber went under and he grappled with his pole. "Dad, I got something!"

For the next several minutes, he reeled in a large rainbow trout. "Way to go!" I laughed, but the sound rang empty in my head. I'd said I'd do what it took to make Chance happy, and I'd meant it.

I hadn't thought it'd cost me my happiness. I'd only been on one date. One spectacular date that nothing else could compare to. I vibed with Scarlett on a level I never had with anyone else. In my gut, I knew she was it.

If I couldn't have her, I wasn't settling for anyone else.

But my kid didn't want her or another woman.

I went through the motions of catching a fish, my mind on my predicament, and took pictures while my insides were a flurry of emotions.

Guilt welled, a hot brand in my stomach. I was with Chance, but I wasn't. Even now, my mind was on Scarlett and me.

It could work. I just needed a chance.

Ironic that was my son's name.

Next, my bobber disappeared.

Chance bounced up and down, pointing. "Dad! Dad!"

"Got it!" Irritated the fish was interrupting some

perfectly good brooding, I reeled in another rainbow trout. This time, Chance took a picture of me and the fish.

I stuffed my thoughts away and concentrated on enjoying my day with my son. We caught two more fish, one for each of us, before packing it in. The meat would be enough for a meal and to freeze.

As we were loading our gear into the truck to head back to the house, I couldn't let it go. I shut the tailgate. "Chance, bud. We've gotta talk."

He turned wide eyes my way, then his shoulders hunched. "It's about her."

"Can we invite her over for supper? She'd love to hear about the fish you caught."

The thought of boasting about his skills to a woman who'd applied constant pressure to live up to his potential must've done it. "Fine. *One* dinner. Cook the smaller fish for her."

The corner of my mouth kicked up. I wanted a shot. I wouldn't chide him about being generous with guests this one time.

Scarlett

An hour ago, I'd received a text with a picture of a beaming Chance with a nice-sized rainbow trout and an invite to come for supper.

He's giving us a shot; that was all the text had said as an explanation.

I had stared at that message for a good ten minutes, thrilled that Tate had lived up to his promise to get ahold of me again.

How hard had he worked to get Chance to agree? Knowing Chance, Tate had piggybacked off the endorphins of the successful catch. I'd done the same thing in the classroom to get Chance to finish assignments.

Once I ripped my gaze off Tate's invite, I had a decision to make. Did I risk Chance's deliberation?

He was a good kid. I was a good teacher. And I was no longer his teacher. He was worried about losing time with his dad. I wanted to spend time with his dad.

Knowing Chance, his two major concerns would be Tate getting stolen from him and me being a domineering taskmaster. I could work with that. Both Tate and I would be considerate of his son as we navigated our own "maybe" relationship.

Could it work?

It had to. Both guys had to get to know me. I'd learn about them and maybe...we could be something. Maybe Tate wouldn't be embarrassed by my needlework or think I was demented because I watched murder shows to relax. He hadn't seemed to. Maybe Chance would trust I had his best interests at heart, even when making him finish book reports.

I'd go.

After Summer and Autumn had left, I'd taken a long bath. My hair was dried and back in a ponytail. I almost redid it, but I left it alone. Chance wasn't impressed by appearances and I didn't want him to think I was trying too hard for his dad. I left on my jean shorts, but I changed out of my Copper Summit Bourbon tee. I couldn't look like a kiss-ass.

Safely tucked into my Montana State shirt, I followed Tate's directions to his place. I knew the area he lived in, and Autumn had brought me out to show me when it was being built, but I was grateful for the guidance, or I would've missed the turnoff from the winding gravel road.

I parked outside the three-car garage. The house had been built the summer before Tate had moved to Bourbon Canyon permanently. My place would fit into half the garage. Was Tate a car guy?

I didn't know much about him, but I felt like I knew him. Was I setting myself up to get hurt?

I'd taken a chance by going through with what had turned out to be the best date of my life. I had to keep going. By the time I got out of the car to admire both the house and the view, Tate was on his large wrap-around porch, his arms braced on the wooden railing. He wasn't wearing a flannel, just a simple black shirt with his rugged jeans and cowboy boots.

Mountain men were so my type. One in particular.

The log cabin was two stories tall, with a large peak cresting over most of the structure. The main area had to be open concept and almost as stunning inside as it was outside, with the view of the valley and the mountains rimming the other side.

"This place is amazing," I said, taking my time crossing to him. My heart thudded. There was still time to chicken out. I could pretend I'd left my oven on or something. But I was here. I was here because it was important to me to try—and because Tate had made an attempt too. I wouldn't get scared off. "That view is ridiculous."

The proud look on his face matched the photo of Chance he'd sent. "When I was a kid, I called dibs on this spot. I didn't think I'd build out here for real."

Then he'd had to move home to take over for his dad. "How's your dad doing?"

He lifted a shoulder. "The cancer's going to take him soon, but he won't stop. I have to get up earlier and earlier to beat him to chores." Fondness crept into his eyes, but it was aimed at me as I crested the porch stairs. "Thanks for coming."

"I couldn't resist the cute invite." I stopped by him, and he brushed the backs of his fingers down my face.

His expression was full of need, like if we had

another overnight, we'd start right where we'd left off before we'd fallen asleep. "He's...resistant to the idea."

I nodded. "Of me."

"No. Well, maybe. But I think he's more scared my time with him will be even more lean. I haven't done the best job proving I've changed."

I gripped his hand. "It takes time." I took another moment to soak in the green valley and towering trees, mostly to fortify my courage. Chance was inside. Was his mind made up?

He leaned in close. "I want to bend you over this railing so bad."

I sucked in a breath. "You have the *worst* timing. I'm going to walk in with a raging blush, and he's going to think I'm trying to trick him into liking me."

"You don't need to trick him. But maybe assure him you can no longer give him extra homework?" He winked and took my hand.

He led me inside. My stomach clambered into my throat with each step. I was more nervous about meeting a kid I already knew than I had been for any job interview.

I didn't want a job. I wanted Tate.

I couldn't focus on the sweeping log ceiling arching high overhead. Or the chic rustic interior. I couldn't admire the space and the style. I searched for a little boy —and a test.

"Hi, Chance." I dropped Tate's hand when I spotted Chance playing video games, tucked deep into a corner couch, his arms propped on his scrawny knees. The TV would be too big for my living room, but the size of this house made it look minuscule.

He only flicked a glance my way, then focused on the

TV. I shook my head at Tate before he could growl at his son's lack of manners.

The old *ignore her and she'll go away* tactic. I had one benefit I hadn't considered until now: I knew this kid. I knew how his brilliant, sometimes devious little mind worked. I knew when he was upset, when he was thinking hard, and when he was truly excited. The photo Tate had sent showed a genuinely happy Chance.

Careful not to appear like I was trying too hard, I said, "Nice trout. Catch anything else?"

Fish talk sparked interest in his eyes. "A walleye."

I glanced at Tate. "Did you get anything?"

"He got two trouts," Chance answered for him. That was a good sign.

"Shore fishing?" I asked.

He nodded.

I stuffed my hands in my pockets. "I spent a lot of my summers fishing with my dad before I left for college."

That snapped his attention off the game, though his gaze was dubious. "You fish?"

"A girl can't fish?" I teased.

Tate was quiet next to me, covering his smile with his hand.

"But you're..."

If he said old, I'd dissolve in a puddle of humiliation. Kids had a way of making me feel ancient when I hadn't even hit my prime.

"A teacher," he finished.

"So were my parents. It's why we could spend all summer at Yellowstone. A couple of years, we went to Glacier for fly-fishing. One time, we even went to my uncle's. He lives outside of Seattle and has a boat. I caught a salmon this big." I held my hands apart...farther than what my catch had actually been. Couldn't help it. I got the trait from my dad.

"No way." He tossed his controller to the side. "Dad's going to get a boat this summer."

"Fishing boat or party boat?"

Tate chuckled.

Chance rolled his eyes. "Fishing, Miss Scarlett."

"We're not at school, Chance. You can just call me Scarlett."

He eyed me. "Do other kids just use your first name?"

"No." I hadn't tried dating their dads either. "Maybe I could, I don't know...go fishing with you guys one time?"

He thought for a moment, his studious gaze jumping from me to his dad. The kid might only be eleven, but he wasn't the same kid who'd walked into my classroom. His teacher next year might have to call one, maybe two, parent meetings, but it wouldn't be all poor-behavior reports.

"It's okay if you don't want me to go." I used my most reassuring tone and gave Tate a look that said I meant it. I wasn't forcing myself on them. "Really. We could just have lemonade at my place." After I took a couple of my wall hangings down.

"It's fine." Chance shrugged. "Dad said we could go next weekend. But, um...is that the same lemonade you brought to school? With the cherries?"

I nodded, biting back a grin. I shamelessly used my lemonade to get to my students' hearts.

"Can you bring that?"

I clamped the inside of my cheek between my teeth

and exchanged a hopeful look with Tate. Pride radiated from the man's handsome face. For me or his kid, I didn't know, and it didn't matter. He hooked his fingers through mine and gave me a grateful squeeze.

"I'll show you how to make it if you want."

He shrugged again and picked up his controller. "I'd rather drink it."

"Okay," I said, chuckling.

Chance glanced at me, surprised.

"It wasn't an assignment, Chance. I'm only a teacher at school, and I'm not even your teacher anymore."

"I know." He looked at his dad. Buried deep in his eyes was the fear he'd lose his dad to me. I didn't have anything to tell him. Only our actions would reassure him. "I'm hungry."

"Want to help me fry the fillets?" Tate asked me. "I haven't started the veggie salad."

Chance groaned.

"The fish are even cleaned already?" I asked, trying to keep the mood playful.

Tate and Chance nodded.

"Well then, count me in. I can chop vegetables with the best of them."

Tate towed me to the kitchen, but I tugged him to a stop. Chance was fiddling with his controller, but he wasn't going back to his game.

"You gonna join us?" I wanted it to sound like an invite and not a job.

Startled, Chance looked up. "I don't know how to cook."

"Want to learn?" Tate asked, his fingers tightening on mine.

"I promise there're no tests or meetings," I added.

"Only good food. Or you can come hang out too, if you want, and tell me about your day."

"Yeah." Chance bounced up and followed us. "Hey, Miss—uh, Scarlett. You think you can show Dad how to make that lemonade?"

"I'll have to swear you both to secrecy." I shot him a grave look. "The other students might find out I use a mix."

He chortled. "Seriously?"

I nodded, and Tate said, "But she adds lemon wedges and cherries."

I leaned down. "Our little secret."

Chance entered the kitchen, grinning. We were all smiling.

I had thought Chance would be harder to win over than Tate, but it turned out these boys weren't like any I'd known before. There might be a lot of fish in the sea, but Tate and Chance Bailey were made for me.

Scarlett

One year later...

"That's the biggest one yet!" I hovered by Chance, ready to jump in at his word. The lake was calm this morning, and the new pontoon Tate had gotten was perfect for relaxing and fishing.

Wind ruffled Chance's hair as he finished reeling in another trout, his second of the day. "Do you see it, Scar? Lookit!"

Tate cradled my hips in his hands as he scooted around me. "Nice job, bud."

Chance brandished the impressive fish. "It's fucking huge."

I rolled my lips in, fighting back the reprimand. I should be used to hearing what we dubbed *fish talk*, but school had just gotten out for the summer and it was hard leaving teacher mode.

I dug my phone out of my linen shorts pocket and took the obligatory photos of Chance and his catch.

A year had passed. The sixth annual bachelor auction had been last night, and neither Tate nor I had had a reason to be there. Tate and Chance had played a video game, and I'd finished a tamer version of my entry embroidery. *Live, Laugh, Hook 'Em Big*. Chance had helped me come up with it.

Today, we continued our one-year celebration by getting the boat on the water. Tate and Chance had gotten a drift boat for fly-fishing a spot they'd found on the river and the pontoon we took to the lake on the far side of the valley that Tate's house overlooked.

Once the fish was secured, Tate glanced at his watch. "We'd better wrap this up and get back."

Wynter and June were in town. They'd gone shopping in Bozeman with Summer and Autumn and were supposed to meet us at Tate's place for supper, along with Teller and Tenor. The guys would bring Tate's parents out.

"Yeah, we'd better wrap up," Chance said, a little too loud, like he was hiding something.

I shot him a perplexed look. He could still be a precocious kid, but it was summer, and he'd had a stellar year in school. When he had issues with his teacher, he'd come to chat with me at recess, and we'd talk through the problems.

So what was he hiding?

When I turned to start packing up my fishing gear, I found Tate on his knees, his tackle box open.

"What are you do—" I gasped.

Tucked in the compartment next to a set of flies was a shiny diamond ring. My gaze flew to Tate's. In my periphery, Chance was shifting from foot to foot, excited.

"Miss Scarlett, will you marry me?"

I put my hand on my chest. My heart hammered. He was proposing. Tate was asking me to marry him. We hadn't talked about it, and I hadn't wanted to assume or to make him feel rushed. He'd been married before, and I was just happy spending time with two of my favorite people and the best family ever.

"Scar?" Chance prompted when I didn't answer.

"Yes. Oh my god, yes." I didn't bother digging the ring out. I carefully set the box on a bench seat and tugged Tate to his feet to hug me.

He planted a kiss on me, full of promise that we'd celebrate much later after Chance was asleep. I curled my hands into the flannel he wore over his standard black shirt. After a few moments, I broke away and reached an arm out to bring Chance into our circle.

"You were in on it," I teased.

He nodded. "Dad and I have been talking."

Tate rubbed my shoulder. "I told him I wanted to marry you and asked how he felt."

"You're cool with me. Wish you'd let me watch your shows with you," he grumbled.

"We'll stick to superhero movies. Serial killer documentaries come later."

He nodded. "How many kids are you going to have?"

"I…" I met Tate's amused gaze, but tucked deep in the depths of those brown irises was a longing that matched mine. We hadn't talked about having kids. I wanted them, but I was afraid to hope Tate was open to more. He and his son had formed a tight bond over the last year. "Do you want more?" I asked softly.

Chance answered first. "I think it'd be cool to be an older brother."

The corner of my mouth lifted, but I hung on Tate's answer.

"Yes," he said simply.

"Really?"

He planted a kiss on my head and ruffled Chance's hair. "I have one awesome kid who's helped me get the hang of this dad thing."

Chance rolled his eyes, but his smile was wide as he turned to dig the ring out of the box for me.

The second he was busy, Tate leaned in, his hot breath wafting over my ear and sending shivers down my spine. "I want to watch your belly grow big with my baby. Does that make me a caveman?"

"It makes you the perfect mountain man. A bourbon bachelor well worth the twenty grand your sisters spent."

Wynter can't let go of her memories of the haunted foster boy who used to read to her, so she hunts down the man he turned into. When she learns jaded Myles Foster won't let anyone get close to him, she gets hired by him instead. The boy who once comforted her might need that little girl to save him now in Bourbon Lullaby.

ABOUT THE AUTHOR

I live the dream in my own slice of paradise where I get to enjoy colorful sunsets from my rocking chair while I'm working. I have my very own romance hero with Mr. Rose and there's more than a few little rose buds running around. A couple aren't so little anymore! We keep things interesting with cats and a dog and the critters that roam though the yard (fingers crossed the mountain lions stay away).

walkerrosebooks.com

ALSO BY WALKER ROSE

Bourbon Canyon Series
Bourbon Bachelor
Bourbon Lullaby
Bourbon Runaway

Printed in Dunstable, United Kingdom